HERE COMES JONATHAN!

BY

CAY M. ANDERSEN

ILLUSTRATED BY
SISTER MARY LANE

PARACLETE PRESS

TO
JENNIFER, PETER, AMY
AND
ALL CHILDREN
LARGE AND SMALL

WRITTEN FOR THEM
BY MI-MI

ILLUSTRATED BY
S. MARY

IN OUR

house

THERE LIVES...

A LITTLE CREATURE.

AND WARM.

HIS NAME IS JONATHAN.

JONATHAN IS WHITE WITH APRICOT COLORED EARS

HE RUNS A LOT
WITH A YELLOW
BALL IN
HIS MOUTH

HIS EARS GO
FLIP FLOP
FLIP FLOP

HE IS FUNNY

SOMETIMES HE
RUNS AND TRIES
TO BARK WITH
HIS YELLOW BALL
IN HIS MOUTH
YIP --- YIP

AND BARKS

IT'S A LOUD
YAP YAP!

HE IS A BIG DOG...

AND IS
GUARDING
HIS MISTRESS'
HOME.

HE IS SO FUNNY
AND CUTE.
WHEN HE SEES
ME HIS LITTLE
TAIL SHAKES

FROM

SIDE

TO

SIDE.

JESUS LOVES JONATHAN.

AND...

I HOPE YOU DO TOO.

THE
END